T0368466

The Christmas Tree Twins

Raymond Hansen Knudsen

AuthorHouse™
1663 Liberty Drive
Bloomington, IN 47403
www.authorhouse.com
Phone: 1 (800) 839-8640

Published by AuthorHouse 09/28/2015

ISBN: 978-1-5049-4726-8 (sc)
ISBN: 978-1-5049-4727-5 (e)

Library of Congress Control Number: 2015914278

authorHOUSE®

Acknowledgements

We extend many thanks to our family and friends. Without your steadfast support and encouragement, the dream of turning this beloved poem into an illustrated story would not have been possible. Because of your earnest love and prayers, "The Christmas Tree Twins" will now be cherished by many families for years to come.

And a special appreciation to granddaughter, Elizabeth Ivy Warwick, for all her dedication and efforts put toward the editing and revision necessary to see this book to completion.

Illustrator, Dana Warwick was inspired by her father's heartfelt poem and brought form and color to the story of the Christmas Tree Twins. Her father's dream was to see his poem in the hands of family and friends becoming part of their Christmas tradition. He was able to see many of the illustrations which he found to be just as he pictured them. She lives in Columbia, South Carolina.

Foreword

One cold wintry day long ago our Papa took a walk to one of his favorite places to admire the beauty of the new fallen snow and the quiet it brings. To our family this special place was called the Grove. It was a wooded area a short distance just beyond the back yard of our time-honored homestead. The Grove was filled with towering old trees and spindly young trees. It was the home of pine, holly, cedar, and oak. There were bushes, briars, and vines of all shapes and sizes.

On this magical day, he walked through the fallen snow, like an explorer looking for hidden treasure. Deep in the Grove, he saw two trees that were almost covered with snow. To him they looked like twin Christmas trees. He looked at them with amazement. Papa appreciated this beautiful sight and was determined to never forget the trees. The trees filled his imagination. The lines of the poem grew one after another into a story of need, kindness, and appreciation. To Papa's delight the poem was finally completed.

Year after year, family and friends would gather with anticipation to hear him recite his Christmas poem. The room would grow quiet as he recited the poem from memory, warming the hearts of all. His hope and dream was that the poem would remain a tradition to brighten Christmas for generations to come. The story of the Christmas Tree Twins is a cherished reminder that the greatest of gifts can be found in the simplest of treasures.

Long long ago, and far far away
in a land where the north winds blow,

there deep in the wood two Christmas trees stood,
with their boughs nearly covered with snow.

All through the night they would wait for the light
that came with the dawn of each day.
And as the hours passed by, their needles would sigh
and the wind their tassels would sway.

Then came the season, and we all know the reason,
two wood cutters came to the site.
For they had searched the long day for just such a display,
as these trees were a revealing delight.

So they were carried away by the means of a sleigh
and placed by the side of a store.

And the people who passed, some were wealthy in class, some were glad, some were sad, some were poor.

As Christmas drew near, there were songs to bring cheer, and candles to give a warm glow.

But the trees thought of the wood and the place where they stood, with their boughs nearly covered with snow.

Then came a young lad who was terribly sad
with his mother, who was shedding great tears.
For theirs had been loss, like a tempest would toss,
with heartaches for so many years.

The man from the store said, "I have a few more,
but these two you may take without price."
For he had seen the lad and knew he was sad,
and wanted to do something nice.

Oh, what a joy to see that dear boy
take hold of those trees with his mother.
Then off they did go, stepping high in the snow
to share with his sisters and brother.

While on the way home, the wind seemed to moan
and the twins in reply gave a sigh.
For their spirit was low with still further to go
and the night with its darkness was nigh.

So few did they meet as they walked down the street,
still the lights in the windows did show.

But the trees longed for the wood and the place where they stood with their boughs nearly covered with snow.

My, what a sight that cold winter's night
when they brought those two trees to the door,
for the children within, each had a big grin
as they jumped up and down on the floor.

Now Mother said, "See, we do have a tree,
in fact they were given to you."
And the boy who was sad said, "Mother, I'm glad,
but what shall we do with two?"

She smiled and said, for she had in her head
a plan for both of the trees:
"We'll give to the poor, the people next door,
for they are in need just as we."

Each was placed in a stand in that far away land,
and trimmed from tip top to toe.
And the children had fun as back and forth they did run
with garland and tinsel and bow.

That Christmas brought joy for each girl and boy
and lifted the spirits of all.
And the twins played their part in everyone's heart
as if they had answered a call.

The moon came out bright that quiet holy night
And through the windows the trees were a glow.

But they remembered the wood and the place where they stood, with their boughs nearly covered with snow.

About the Author

Raymond Hansen Knudsen (1924-2013) expressed his love for life, family and friends in the positive way he approached life. He was known for his thankfulness and desire to uplift others. He was the author of a collection of poems which capture his experiences of growing up in America. He was a World War II veteran. He called his poems "picture poems" written so descriptively that he hoped the reader would be able to picture each line through their own perspective. He lived in New Jersey most of his life until moving to South Carolina which served as an inspiration for many more poems.

Printed in the United States
By Bookmasters